STEM Superstars

Temple Grandin

by Rachel Castro

Cover: Grandin has worked hard to help people and animals.

Norwood House Press
Chicago, Illinois

For information regarding Norwood House Press, please visit our website at: www.norwoodhousepress.com or call 866-565-2900.

PHOTO CREDITS: Cover: © JC Olivera/Sipa USA/AP Images; © DCA/Michael Carpenter/WENN/Newscom, 21; © Eric Seidle/Havre Daily News/AP Images, 17; © Gregory Rec/Portland Press Herald/Getty Images, 10;© Jack Kurtz UPI Photo Service/Newscom, 13; © Jordan Strauss/Invision for The Gentle Barn/AP Images, 18; © Kim Shiflett/NASA/Sipa USA/Newscom, 14; © Marcio Jose Bastos Silva/Shutterstock Images, 5; © patat/iStockphoto, 9; © raulbaenacasado/Shutterstock Images, 6

Hardcover ISBN: 978-1-68450-922-5
Paperback ISBN: 978-1-68404-458-0

© 2020 by Norwood House Press.

All rights reserved.

No part of this book may be reproduced without written permission from the publisher.

Library of Congress Cataloging-in-Publication Data
Names: Castro, Rachel, author.
Title: Temple Grandin / by Rachel Castro.
Description: Chicago, Illinois : Norwood House Press, [2020] | Series: STEM superstars | Audience: K to Grade 3. | Includes index.
Identifiers: LCCN 2018054274 (print) | LCCN 2018055782 (ebook) | ISBN 9781684044634 (ebook) | ISBN 9781684509225 (hardcover) | ISBN 9781684044580 (paperback)
Subjects: LCSH: Grandin, Temple--Juvenile literature. | Animal scientists--United States--Biography--Juvenile literature. | Autism--Patients--Biography--Juvenile literature.
Classification: LCC SF33.G67 (ebook) | LCC SF33.G67 C37 2020 (print) | DDC 636.0092 [B] --dc23
LC record available at https://lccn.loc.gov/2018054274

319N–072019
Manufactured in the United States of America in North Mankato, Minnesota.

★ Table of Contents ★

Chapter 1
Early Life 4

Chapter 2
Young Inventor 8

Chapter 3
Animal Scientist 16

Career Connections 22
Glossary 23
For More Information 23
Index 24
About the Author 24

Chapter 1

Early Life

Temple Grandin was born in Boston, Massachusetts, in 1947. She could not speak until she was four years old. She has **autism**. Autism can make it hard to speak. There are many kinds of autism.

 Grandin grew up in the Boston, Massachusetts area.

Animals, such as mice, need all of their senses.

> **Did You Know?**
> Grandin's mother was a singer, writer, and actress.

Grandin loved animals. Animals depend on their **senses**. Smells and sounds are important to them. Senses were also important to Grandin. She had trouble with words.

Chapter 2

Young Inventor

School was hard for Grandin. She did not know how to make friends. She learned differently from other students.

 Being different from others can be hard.

Grandin has spent a lot of time with animals.

Grandin visited her aunt. Her aunt lived on a ranch. Grandin worked with cows and horses there. She saw a **squeeze chute** that holds animals still. It gave her an idea.

Grandin invented a hug machine when she was in high school. The hug machine squeezed her like a squeeze chute. It made her feel calm.

 A squeeze chute applies pressure to an animal to help calm them. Grandin applied this concept to her hug machine.

As a professor, Grandin talks to many people.

Did You Know? Grandin also runs her own company.

Grandin did not let autism hold her back. She studied animal science. She earned high **degrees**.

Chapter 3

Animal Scientist

Grandin started working with **cattle**. She would be the only woman on the ranch. She knew she had to work hard.

 Grandin has made a huge impact on the cattle industry. She designed better ways to move cattle.

She wanted to make farm animals feel less scared. She made better chutes that helped animals feel safer. Her goal was to make them feel calm.

When animals feel safe, the workers are safer, too.

Did You Know?
A movie was made about Grandin's life. It was called Temple Grandin.

Grandin helps people and animals. Her autism helped her understand animals. She is an **advocate** for people with autism. She has written many books. She writes about animals and autism.

 Grandin has written many books that have helped lots of people.

★ Career Connections ★

1. When she was young, Grandin visited her aunt's ranch and got to work with cows and horses. Ask an adult if there's a nearby farm you can visit. At some farms, visitors help feed the animals.

2. If you have a classroom pet, volunteer to care for it. If you've never cared for an animal before, ask your teacher to help you learn about it.

3. Grandin had trouble in school. She eventually joined a robotics club and an electronics club. She also began horseback riding. What clubs or after-school activities does your school offer that may help you find your strengths?

4. Once you're old enough, consider volunteering at an animal shelter. It might help you decide if you want to work with animals in the future.

5. 4-H is a nonprofit for kids interested in animal science and farming. It helps kids with hands-on learning. See if there's a 4-H club in your community.

★ Glossary ★

advocate (ad-vuh-KIT): Someone who fights for something or someone.

autism (AW-tiz-um): A set of behavioral issues that affects a person's ability to communicate; people with autism are often sensitive to sounds, lights, or touch.

cattle (KAT-uhl): Cows or bulls raised for meat or milk.

degrees (di-GREEZ): An honor that a person earns after finishing college.

senses (SENSS-iz): The ways a person or animal experiences the world around them including sight, smell, hearing, taste, and touch.

squeeze chute (SKWEEZ SHEWT): A narrow tunnel that holds animals still.

★ For More Information ★

Books

Joanne Mattern. *Farm Animals*. Washington, DC: National Geographic, 2017. This book shows readers photographs of farm animals and provides information about them.

Rebecca Felix. *Temple Grandin*. Minneapolis, MN: Abdo Publishing, 2017. This book shows readers what Grandin has done in the cattle industry.

Websites

AIPL Kid's Corner: Facts about Cows
(https://www.aipl.arsusda.gov/kc/cowfacts.html) This page contains facts and information about cows for kids.

Sesame Street: Explaining Autism
(https://sesamestreetincommunities.org/topics/autism/?utm_source=google&utm_medium=cpc&utm_term=autismwebsites&utm_content=AutismWebsites&utm_campaign=SSIC2018) This page contains a video and activities that explain autism.

★ Index ★

A
Advocate, 20
Autism, 4, 15, 20

B
Boston, Massachusetts, 4

C
Cattle, 16

H
Hug machine, 12

R
Ranch, 11, 16

S
School, 8, 12
Squeeze chute, 11–12

★ About the Author ★

Rachel Castro is a Minneapolis-based writer. She holds degrees in English literature and creative nonfiction. In addition to writing for the educational market, she works for a public library and teaches creative writing.